Rita and the Flying Saucer

Hilda Offen

Happy Cat Books

For Alice

HAPPY CAT BOOKS

Published by Happy Cat Books Ltd.
Bradfield, Essex CO11 2UT, UK

First published 2003
1 3 5 7 9 10 8 6 4 2

Copyright © Hilda Offen, 2003
The moral right of the author/illustrator has been asserted
All rights reserved

A CIP catalogue record for this book is available from the British Library

ISBN 1 903285 64 X

Printed in China by Midas Printing Limited

"Look at those lights!" said Eddie. "What do
you think they are?"
"Shooting stars!" said Julie.
"Lightning!" said Jim.
"Perhaps it's a spaceship," said Rita.
"RITA! DON'T BE SILLY!" they shouted.

The next day Eddie, Julie and Jim jumped on their skateboards.

"We're going to investigate," said Eddie. "We think a spaceship landed last night."

"I said that!" said Rita. "Can I come?"

"No, you can't," said Julie. "Why don't you stay in and watch the Tubbly-Bubblies?"

Rita stamped indoors and switched on the television. The screen flickered and a strange face appeared.

"Greetings from the Planet Norma Alpha," it said.

"Ho-hum!" said Rita. "More work for the Rescuer."

And she changed into her outfit and whizzed out of the window.

Outside in the street some Norms were
approaching a litter-bin.
"Can I help?" asked Rita.

"No!" they said. "Go away. You're much too small."

ZOOM

"Please yourselves!" said Rita and she moved so quickly the Norms were left blinking.

"Hallo!" said Rita as she flew over the allotments. "I spy trouble."
A Norm was trying to steal Mr McGregor's prize marrow.

"DROP THAT MARROW!"

Rita's roar was so fierce that Mr McGregor
and the Norm fell backwards.
Mr McGregor landed in a bed of marigolds
but the Norm fell into the compost heap.
"Ugh!" he said. "I'm off!" and he
scrambled out and flew away
into the distance.

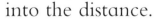

"You've got an amazing roar, Rescuer!" said
Mr McGregor.
"Thank you!" said Rita. "Uh-oh! I'm
needed at the supermarket."

"Stop, thieves!" yelled Mr
Biggins. "They're stealing
my cornflakes!"
"And they've got our
skateboards!" screamed
Julie and Jim.

Rita ran like an antelope. She leaped on the back of the skateboards and the Norms shot in the air.

"Now hand over those cornflakes!" said Rita.

"Not likely!" said the Norms and they raised their deadly jelly guns.

13

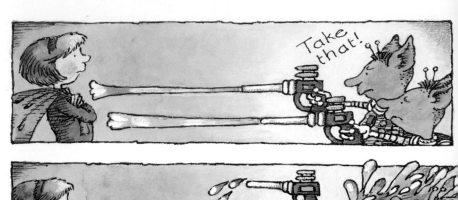

"Boing!" The jelly bounced off Rita's chest and shot back at the Norms. "Splat!" They were covered from head to toe.

"Help!" cried little Lucy Gill as the Norms squelched away. "There's some more of them! They've got Tigger, my hamster!"

14

Oh no! The Norms weren't
looking where they were going.
They were heading straight for
a helicopter!

Rita didn't hesitate. She zoomed after the jet-scooter, seized the controls and steered it out of harm's way.
"Look where you're going in future," she said. "That could have been very nasty."

Then she grabbed Tigger and took him back to Lucy; but she had no time for a breather.

"Rescuer!" screamed a little boy. "There's an alien in the playground. He's going round and round on the swings!"

Sure enough, there on a swing was a little
Norm. His jet-pack had jammed and he
was whizzing round like a windmill.
Rita caught the swing and hung on till it
stopped. A plume of smoke rose in the air.
"Boo-hoo!" wept the little Norm. "It's too
far to walk back to the flying saucer. I'm
lost!"

"There, there!" said Rita. "Where did you leave the saucer?"

"Don't know!" sobbed the Norm. "There were tall posts with green stuff on top. And small furry beings with long ears."

"Hm!" said Rita. "Those sound like trees. And rabbits. I think you're talking about Foxley Wood. Come on!"

"We're too late!" cried the Norm as they reached the wood. "They're taking off!"

Quick— let's get out of here!

19

He was right! All the jet-scooters were
returning to the flying saucer. Worse still,
Eddie was in one of them.

"Help!" he screamed as the doors slammed
shut.

Rita picked up an abandoned space-helmet.
"Put this on!" she said. "We've no time to
lose!"

They shot upwards and after a
while they saw the flying
saucer ahead of them.
Rita rapped on the window.
"Open the air-lock!" gasped
the captain.

"Mum!"

"It's my
little Zark! I
wondered where
he was."

"Why have you kidnapped that boy? And that cat? And that pig?" asked Rita. "And what are you doing with those chips?"
"We are running short of our special food, the Googoo fruit," said the captain. "We had hoped to survive on your earth food. But we cannot eat it."

"And we are lost!" said his second-in-command. "We are trying to find a clever earthling who can find the way home for us."
"But it's hopeless!" said the captain. "So far they have scored nought out of ten."
"Test me!" said Rita; so they did.
"Ten out of ten!" cried the Norms. "What a brain!"

"Not even our wisest old Norm can find the
way home on the star chart," said the
captain. "Will you take a look?"
"With pleasure," said Rita. "Aha! An easy
enough mistake. You were holding the map
upside down. There's Norma Alpha."
"But it is a thousand light years away!" said
the captain. "We only have enough Googoo
fruit for a week."

"I know a short cut," said Rita. "There you are! That should only take you two or three days."

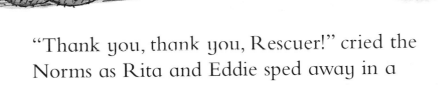

"Thank you, thank you, Rescuer!" cried the Norms as Rita and Eddie sped away in a jet-scooter, along with the cat and the pig.

Go carefully!

You can keep the jet-scooter.

"Nearly home!" said Rita.
"Oh no – more trouble!"
An asteroid was heading
for earth.

"POW!" Rita shattered it by flying at it with her head. It fell to earth in a shower of stardust.

27

Down on the Sports Field hordes of people had gathered. There were TV cameras and reporters amongst them.
Rita landed the jet-scooter and everyone cheered.

"They're all yours!" Rita said to the
reporters. "I have to go!"

"Still watching TV, Rita?" asked Julie later on that night. "You'll get square eyes."

"You missed the Rescuer again!" cried Jim.

"I was abducted by aliens!" said Eddie. "The Rescuer saved me! And she saved the earth from being hit by an asteroid."

"I know!" said Rita. "I've seen it all on the News."

Rita the Rescuer

When you are the youngest in the family, you can sometimes get left out of the fun. Then one day Rita Potter is sent a magical Rescuer's outfit which gives her amazing powers... Three cheers for Rita!

Arise, Our Rita!

Rita may be the youngest of the Potter family, but she also is the fabulous Rescuer! And teaching archery to Robin Hood, taming dragons and giants, is all in a day's work for our pint-sized superhero.

Rita and the Romans

Left behind in the Potter family's Wendy-house it is lucky Rita has her Rescuer's outfit to hand. In no time at all she rescuing toddlers, saving gladiators and even building Adrian's Wall!

Rita at Rushybrook Farm

A visit to Rushybrook Farm is a great treat. Unless you've been left in the Little Pets Barn with the babies. Rita the Rescuer has other ideas, however, and soon is lifting pigs out of mud, stopping runaway caravans and generally having an action-packed day!